BUNNIES IN A SLEIGH

A CRAZY CHRISTMAS STORY!

by Philip Ardagh and Ben Mantle

WALKER BOOKS
AND SUBSIDIARIES
LONDON · BOSTON · SYDNEY · AUCKLAND

For Father Christmas. Thank you — P. A.

For my bouncy little bunnies, Milo and Felix — B. M.

First published 2023 by Walker Books Ltd, 87 Vauxhall Walk, London SE11 5HJ ∗ Text © 2023 Philip Ardagh ∗ Illustrations © 2023 Ben Mantle
The right of Philip Ardagh and Ben Mantle to be identified as the author and illustrator respectively of this work has been asserted in accordance
with the Copyright, Designs and Patents Act 1988 ∗ This book has been typeset in Archer Book ∗ Printed in China ∗ All rights reserved ∗ No
part of this book may be reproduced, transmitted or stored in an information retrieval system in any form or by any means, graphic, electronic
or mechanical, including photocopying, taping and recording, without prior written permission from the publisher. ∗ British Library Cataloguing in
Publication Data: a catalogue record for this book is available from the British Library ∗ ISBN 978-1-5295-0712-6 ∗ www.walker.co.uk ∗ 10 9 8 7 6 5 4 3 2 1

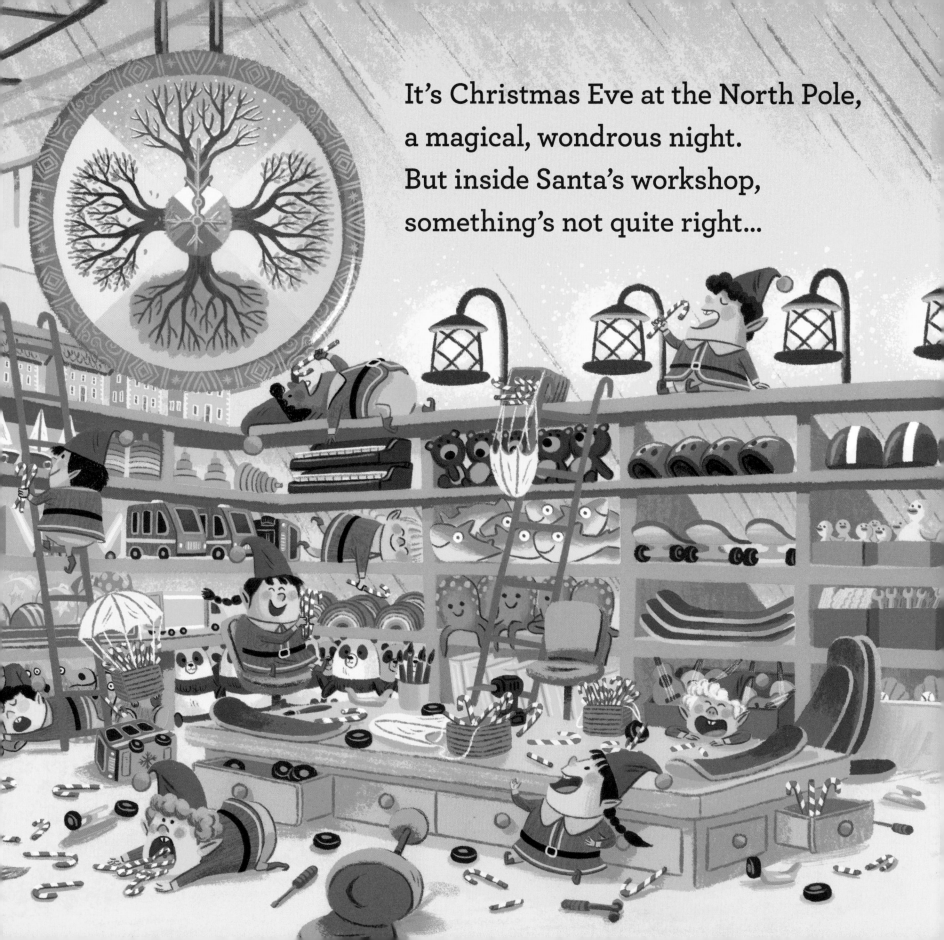

It's Christmas Eve at the North Pole,
a magical, wondrous night.
But inside Santa's workshop,
something's not quite right...

The elves are eating candy canes.
Their tiny tummies swell!

Far too many sugary treats
have made them MOST unwell.

Chief Elf is in PANIC MODE,
letting out a worried yelp!
So little time, so much to do.
Poor Santa will need help!

What the jingle-bells is happening in the glistening snow outside?

It's some
Christmas-crazy bunnies
on a frantic dog-pulled ride!

The bunnies are excited!
They've found their friend, first try.
(The one who gave out candy canes!)
And now – it's time to FLY!

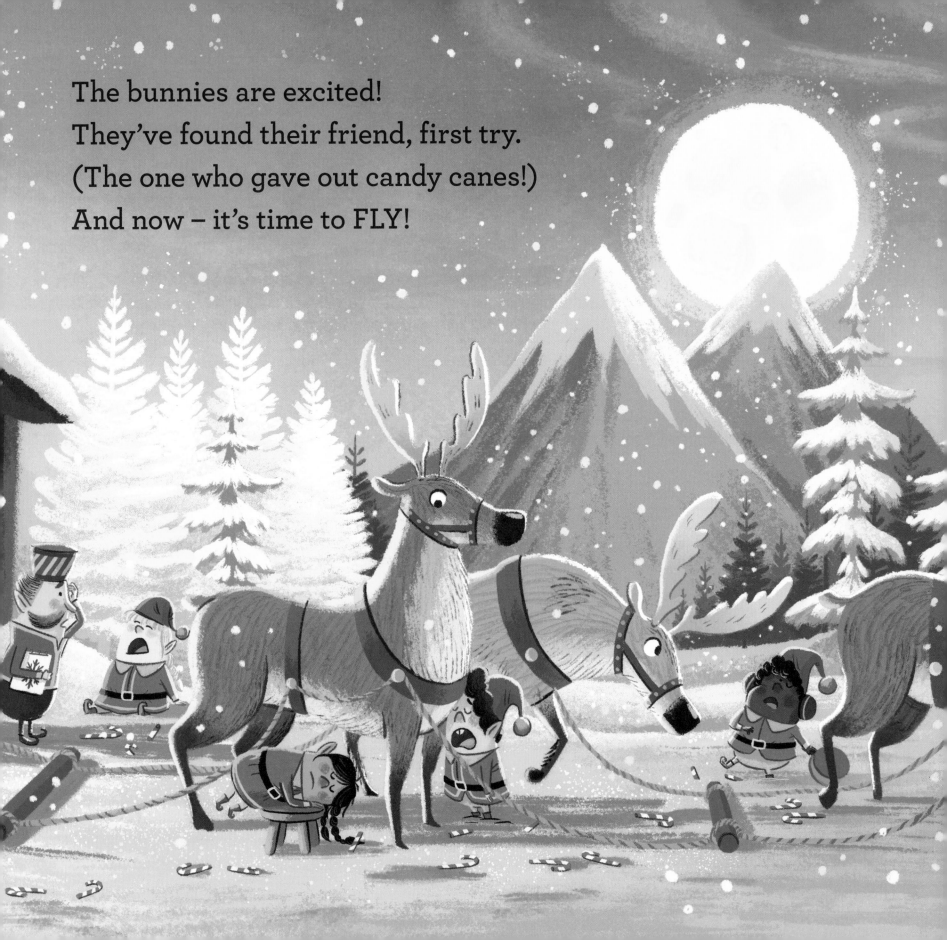

The reindeer
are on standby.

Rudolph's nose lights
up for GO!

The sleigh is cleared
for take-off
as they run across
the snow!

Bunnies in a sleigh!
Bunnies in a sleigh!

Laughing and a-joking
as they head for Christmas Day!

High up on a rooftop,
the bunnies land on tiles.
One leaps down
a chimney...

Now she's sooty,
and all smiles!

She's followed by the others.
They all look SUCH a mess!
Telling which of them is which
is impossible to guess.

Bunnies in the house!

Bunnies in the house!

Popping presents everywhere.

Here's one for Mrs Mouse!

Bunnies all aboard again,
each on a reindeer's back.
But what is Santa up to?
Sorting presents from his sack!

Clock tower up ahead!
Clock tower up ahead!

PHEW! The sleigh just missed it ...

but hit a Christmas
tree instead!

Out fall all the presents,
and then the bunnies, too!

There's no time
to be wasted.

There's still so much to do!

Bunnies in a sleigh!

Bunnies in a sleigh!

Laughing and a-joking
as they head for Christmas Day!

Bunnies stuck
in chimneys!

Bunnies stuck
in snow!

Bunnies stuffed in stockings!

And caught up in mistletoe!

Kissy! Kissy!

The stockings are all filled now.
The end of night is near.

It's time to head back to the Pole,
and the bunnies give a CHEER!

"HOOOOOORAY!"

With the presents all delivered,
Santa's in a jolly mood.
As for those funny bunnies?

They're all sharing reindeer food!
"HO HO HO!"

"MERRY CHRISTMAS, EVERYONE!"